Felix & Alexander

Terry Denton

APR 3 '90

Houghton Mifflin Company
Boston 1988

Alexander lived in a block of flats in the big city. Even though he was not allowed to have a real pet, he had Felix, a toy dog. Felix was Alexander's best friend and always laughed at Alexander's jokes.

Every afternoon Alexander would go for a walk in the city streets near his block of flats. He couldn't take Felix because he was too small. Felix would sit up at the window, waiting for Alexander to return.

One afternoon Alexander did not return home from his walk at his usual time. Felix waited and waited and became very worried. He decided that Alexander must be lost.

Felix had to find Alexander. He packed his torch into his suitcase and went out to look for Alexander.

Felix climbed out of the window, edged across to the drainpipe and slid down in to the garden.

As Felix slipped out through a hole in the garden fence, a nail tore his side. Tiny balls of stuffing like pale pink pearls fell from the tear. Clutching his side, Felix ran into the street.

Night was falling and the air was becoming colder. Would Felix ever find his best friend Alexander?

As he wandered through the streets the houses seemed to grow taller. Felix felt scared and very small.

Suddenly Felix heard a scream. It was Alexander, in the grip of a fearsome monster!

Felix quickly unpacked his torch and shone it at Alexander and the monster. The monster turned to stone under the bright beam of light.

Felix had saved Alexander, but they now had to find their way home. The two friends were both lost. Through the dark and endless streets they walked, the torchlight their only guide.

After a long time they sat down to rest. To cheer Felix up, Alexander told a joke. While he was waiting for Felix to finish laughing, he noticed something sparkling slightly in the torchlight. It was Felix's stuffing.

Felix had been leaking ever since he'd torn his side on the nail in the garden fence, and had accidentally made a trail that would now lead Felix and Alexander all the way home.

Very soon Felix and Alexander were standing at the front door of their block of flats.

After giving him some new extra stuffing, Alexander sewed up the little tear in Felix's side while promising never to get lost again. The two friends climbed into bed and were soon fast asleep.

For a long time after, Felix would always feel a little stitch in his side when he laughed too hard at Alexander's jokes, and he would remember their adventure in the streets of the city.

For Rita Scharf